I0615543

George Monck Berkeley

Heloise

Or the siege of Rhodes. A legendary tale. Vol. 1

George Monck Berkeley

Heloise
Or the siege of Rhodes. A legendary tale. Vol. 1

ISBN/EAN: 9783337393168

Printed in Europe, USA, Canada, Australia, Japan

Cover: Foto ©Andreas Hilbeck / pixelio.de

More available books at **www.hansebooks.com**

HELOISE:

OR, THE

SIEGE OF RHODES.

A

LEGENDARY TALE.

BY THE AUTHOR OF

MARIA: OR, THE GENEROUS RUSTIC.

SECOND EDITION.

TO WHICH IS ADDED,

HARRIET:

OR, THE VICAR'S TALE.

Fierce Wars, and faithful Loves, fhall moralize my Song.

Spencer's Proeme to the Fairy Queen.

IN TWO VOLUMES.

VOL. I.

LONDON:

For J. FORBES, C. ELLIOT and T. KAY, P. M'QUEEN,
T. and J. EGERTON, SHEPPERDSON and
REYNOLD, C. STALKER; C. RANN,
Oxford; TODD, York; and
C. ELLIOT, Edinburgh.

M.DCC.LXXXVIII.

TO THE HONORABLE

M R s. *WARD,*

ARE THESE VOLUMES

RESPECTFULLY INSCRIBED,

BY

HER OBLIGED AND VERY

OBEDIENT HUMBLE SERVANT,

THE AUTHOR.

ADVERTISEMENT

TO THE

SECOND EDITION.

———

THE AUTHOR cannot suffer a Second Edition to appear, without expressing the gratitude he feels for the very flattering marks of approbation with which the SIEGE of RHODES has been honored by the Public.

INNER TEMPLE,
April 2, 1788.

P R E F A C E.

ALTHOUGH the candour with which the Author's former attempts have been received, has served, in some degree, to dissipate those apprehensions, inseparable from the breast of him who presumes to attract the public attention ; yet (he flatters himself) it has by no means lessened his anxiety to please.

me

Some years having now elapsed since the writing of the Generous Ruſtic *and the* Spaniſh Memoirs*, *he is well aware that a more finiſhed performance than either of* them *may now be expeɛted; both* thoſe *works were the produɛlions of very early years, and their errors are ſuch as gene-rally mark the unchaſtiſed effuſions of a young author.*

As this is the laſt *time the author will ever expoſe himſelf to criticiſm, (in the*

---

* Although accident delayed, for a conſiderable time, the publication of this work, yet it was written ſhortly after the Generous Ruſtic.

charaɛter

character of a novelist) he has been parti-
cularly affiduous to merit a continuation of
that indulgence he has hitherto experienced.

The fenfelefs farrago that daily iffues
from the prefs, through the medium of
novels, has created in the minds of many
readers a prejudice againft this fpecies
of writing; poffibly, however, on enquiry, the public may find in themfelves
the caufe of this evil. An eftimate of the
literary tafte of any age, can commonly beft
be formed from the nature of thofe publica-
tions with which it abounds.

The

The authors of superficial *novels (however* deservedly *they may fail in their attempts to reach the goal of Fame) are* sure, *amongst the fair inhabitants of every country town in England, to find a numerous host of readers; and from the liberal support they never fail to afford authors of this class, some* profit *at* least *is sure to arise; and* that *must necessarily be considered as the* summum bonum *of those literary drudges, who from the* exalted *situations to which their fortune* confines *them, shower down voluminous memoirs of* cruel fathers, reformed rakes, *and* constant lovers; *the nature and tendency*

dency of which works are to weaken the judgment, and to excite in the minds of the softer sex a dangerous sensibility, from which effects the most funeste have frequently arisen : precluded as are many readers of this description from a general observation of men and manners, they naturally form their ideas of both, from the representations of the novelist ; and these are too frequently unjust. The consequences of these misrepresentations are often fatal to happiness, and there is little doubt that many an amiable woman has embittered her days by adopting the ideas, and by following the example of a

Lucinda,

Lucinda, or a Leonora: fathers who have only wished to restrain imprudence, or protect unsuspecting innocence, have been deserted, whilst the arms *of* a libertine *have been chosen, as affording the properest assylum for one who suffered under an* imaginary *tyranny. On the other hand, the novelist who inculcates the practice of* virtue, *and whose representations of life are* faithful, *may often essentially serve the cause of virtue, and promote the happiness of the* many, *who will receive instruction through* no other *vehicle; a novelist is often received, where the* dignified remonstrances *of* a Sherlock, *and the all eloquent com-*

position

(vi)

position of a White * *would never find admission.*

It is, however, by no means the author's intention to arraign, univerfally,
the tafte of an age that has received,
with unbounded applaufe, the writings of
a Richardfon, a Fielding, a Graves,
a Mac Kenzie, a Burney, a Reeve,
and a Lee, nor would there be any
impropriety in clofing this catalogue
with a name dignified by the practice of every human virtue; but the au-

---

* Of this gentleman it may juftly be faid, that
talents like his have feldom been allotted to
man.

thor

thor of Raffelas has left few who are equal to the task which juftice *requires from the panegyrift of* Johnfon: *to thofe who have perufed the* leaden volume * *lately*

---

* The Author underftanding that fome people have confidered this paffage as alluding to Mrs. Piozzi, thinks it incumbent on him not to neglect the opportunity afforded him by the appearance of a Second Edition, thus publicly to teftify the refpect he entertains for that Lady, of whofe talents he has a *juft*, and *confequently* a *high* opinion; and though *her* Memoirs of Johnsons are by no means faultlefs, they are neither fcandalous nor ftupid.

Thofe, who thus mifapplied the paffage in queftion, have, it is plain, *hitherto efcaped* the perufal of that *comprehenfive libel* publifhed under the title of *Johnfon's Life*. If the Anthor of that performance *ever* poffeffed any portion of candour, it has vanifhed " like the bafelefs fabric of a vifion, and left not a wreck behind."

con-

consecrated to his memory, the recollection
of the following line may possibly occur,

" Fools will rush in, where Angels dare not tread."

To some persons the heroic exertions of
virtue, recorded in the following pages,
may possibly appear unnatural; but the
reader should remember that Heloife and
Montmorin lived in the age of chivalry,
which (however the enthusiasm it inspired,
might some time terminate in folly) was
always the friend of virtue.

To such as may, on perusing this pre-
face be inclined to charge the author with
arro-

arrogance, he begs leave to obferve, that his remarks relate only to the tendency, *and are by no means extended to the* execution *of modern novels;---where the* former *of thefe is reprehenfible,* no *mercy fhould be fhewn---the* patron *of vice, is the* deftroyer *of happinefs;---but he who fails* only *in the* latter, *is furely entitled to fome portion of indulgence.*

How far the author of Heloife *may merit the protection he now folicits, muft be determined by the public, whofe award he awaits with refpectful diffidence.*

Oxford,

Dec. 21, 1787.

C O N T E N T S

O F

V O L U M E I.

C H A P. I.

P A G E I.

a   C H A P.

C H A P. II,

P A G E 9.

Montmorin *receives a meſſage from
the* King, *ſignifying his intentention of
viſiting the Caſtle, in his tour through
the Province. He arrives. Falls in
love with* Heloiſe. *The jealouſy it
occaſions in* Montmorin. *She feigns
indiſpoſition.*

C H A P.

C H A P. III.

P A G E 17.

The King's *disappointment at He-*
loife not appearing. He consults with
Frontin, *his favourite, and agrees that*
he shall feign an indifposition to re-
main at the Caftle. The King *de-*
parts. Montmorin *receives a letter*
from him, offering him the command
of his troops. Confults with Heloife.
She perfuades him to accept it.

C H A P. IV.

P A G E 28.

Heloife *fets off for her Aunt, ac-companied by* Montmorin, *who leaves her there. He embarks for* Rhodes. *The* King *returns to the Caftle. Is enraged at not finding* Heloife *there. Sends orders to all the feaports to prevent her efcape.*

C H A P.

C H A P. V.

P A G E 36.

The King *caufes all the Convents to be fearched, under a pretence of looking for the daughter of* D'Annois. Heloife *is by this means difcovered. She refolves to fet off for* Rhodes.

a 3   C H A P.

C H A P. VI.

P A G E 48.

Heloife *fets off difguifed as a Minftrel for the neareft feaport, and there
embarks for* Rhodes. *Is driven back.
Meets with* D'Anois, *who endeavours
to perfuade her to accompany him to
the* King. *She not confenting, he in-
tends to make her by force.*

C H A P.

(vii)

CHAP. VII.

PAGE 61.

Heloife *effects* her *efcape*. Em-
barks on board a veffel for Rhodes.

CHAP. VIII.

PAGE 68.

Some acount of the Siege of Rhodes.

a 4   CHAP.

C H A P.

C H A P. XI.

P A G E 101.

Montmorin *fold for a flave.* His *adventure with a Turk in the garden.* His *efcape.*

CON-

CONTENTS

OF

VOLUME II.

———

her on board of a veſſel bound for France.

CHAP. XIII.

PAGE 12.

Heloiſe *recovers the uſe of her reaſon. She arrives in* France. *She enquires about* Montmorin. *Is informed that he is dead. Reſolves to ſpend the remainder of her life in a Convent.*

CHAP.

CHAP.

C H A P.

They

H E L O I S E:

OR, THE

SIEGE OF *RHODES.*

A

LEGENDARY TALE.

CHAP. I.

AT a time, when enthusiasm, re-
religious and military, was at its
height, and, with united powers, pro-
moted the spirit of *Crusade*; HUGH
DE MONTMORIN, alike insensible to

B   the

the allurements of martial glory, and the thunders of the Vatican, remained tranquil within the limits of this paternal territory; thus facrificing to the duties of domeftic life that ardent paffion for military atchievement, to which his youthful breaft was by no means a ftranger.

His mother, LAURA DE MONTMO-RIN (by the untimely death of her hufband, who had fallen in fingle combat with a neighbouring Baron) was left furrounded by a numerous family, and expofed to an encreafing hoft of formidable diftreffes. Her caftle lay near to that of the Baron, who had deprived her

her of her Lord; nor did the refent-
ments of VALLANCE, fleep in the grave
of MONTMORIN.

In those days of femi-barbarifm, the
fword of *chivalry* (which the inimitable
DON QUIXOTE has for ever fheathed)
was found a neceffary auxiliary to the
fword of *juftice*; and the monarch himfelf, (becaufe unaided by the genius of
romance) frequently found that the in-
folence of ufurping vaffals made his
throne to totter.

LAURA's mind was well aware of
all the dangers infeparable from her
fituation, and to *her* intreaties was it
owing

owing that the young Baron made a determination *not* to leave her defence-lefs and unprotected in fo perilous a neighbourhood. His retirement there-fore although *inactive,* was by no means *inglorious.*

In thofe unpolifhed times, a ftate of rural elegant fociety, fuch as *we* enjoy, was *abfolutely* unknown; and neighbour-ing Nobles had little intercourfe, but *merely* fuch as mutual fafety required, or as a defire to reftrain regal power occafioned.

Thus circumftanced, HUGH DE MONTMORIN could not feek the fweets
of

of focial intercourfe, beyond the limits of his paternal caftle, within which narrow circle was a young woman, trained up under the kindeft protection of his family, daughter of a gentleman who (having borne arms under the father of the youthful Baron) fell in the Plains of PALESTINE; leaving his only child to his patron's care. Of this important truft the noble guardian acquitted himfelf moft generoufly, educating his lovely ward as his own daughters were educated, and, (by his will) allotting her a portion equal to that he bequeathed to each of his own younger children.

He-

HELOISE was now in her feventeenth year, her figure elegant, her features *not* correctly framed according to the ftatuary's eftablifhed rules, but her bewitching countenance was marked with an expreffion, *interefting in the extreme.* Two perfons of different fexes, and of nearly the fame age, and who *neceffarily* pafs much of their time together, feldom continue *long* in a ftate of indifference with refpect to each other: it is with *people* as with *plants*, moft of them have fecret qualities, good and bad, which are difcovered, only, by intimate acquaintance.

The

The friendſhip between HUGH DE MONTMORIN, and his fair inmate, had naturally ripened into that pure love, which lies concealed at the bottom of the heart; and, for a time, is not known even to ourſelves. A *mutual* attachment could not, however, remain for any length of time, a ſecret to either party; there being no diſguiſe which can long conceal love where it is, or feign it where it is not: in thoſe days the forms of courtſhip were, in general, tedious and diſguſtingly ceremonious; but the ſituation of this happy pair ſuperſeded every thing of this nature; and an unequi-

vocal

vocal avowal of mutual love, foon took place. MONTMORIN, however, (apprehenfive that a connection fo little fplendid might not meet the ideas of of his family) determined on keeping his attachment fecret for the prefent : meanwhile he continued to enjoy the delightful opportunities, afforded by his circumftances, of breathing his vows at the feet of HELOISE, who (fuperior to artifice) attempted not to conceal the pleafure fhe received from his addreffes.

C H A P.

MONTMORIN had hitherto experienced *only the sweets of Love,* a passion, which, the moment it ceases to hope or to fear, ceases to exist: Were we to judge of love by *most* of its effects, we should think it resembled hatred more than kindness. To the passion of jealousy the breast of MONT-MORIN had been hitherto a stranger; for although its birth is *always* coeval with that of love, yet it never discovers itself, itfelf, until called forth by fome danger, real or imaginary. ¯

Whilft MONTMORIN and his HE-LOISE were enjoying the pleafures arifing from a virtuous and unreferved attachment, he received a meffage from his Sovereign, notifying his intention to vifit the caftle of MONT-MORIN, in his tour through the Province.

The various preparations neceffary on fo important, and (in thofe days) uncommon an event, having entirely engroffed the attention of the Baron, the idea of a royal *rival* had never prefented

itfelf

itfelf to his imagination. On the appointed day the monarch and his train arrived. The mother and fifters of MONTMORIN, with the too lovely HELOISE, were prefented to the Sovereign, who received them, *not only* gracioufly, but with all the obliging attentions to which they had fo juft a claim.

No fooner had the King obferved the blufhing HELOISE, than his whole foul was abforbed in the idea of being poffeffed of her incomparable charms. Having (as haftily as he could with propriety) partaken of the fumptuous banquet prepared for him,

the

the love-fick Prince retired to his ap-
partment, where, as foon as he found
himfelf with no other attendance than
his confidential fervant, FRONTIN, *to
him* the important fecret was commu-
nicated. To this faithful domeftic he
gave it in charge, that he fhould en-
deavour to learn every particular re-
lating the fair object of his wifhes.
FRONTIN burned with impatience to
merit his mafter's thanks, and flew
from the royal prefence in queft of intelligence. MONTMORIN *alfo* retired to
his aparment, but with fuch apprehenfions of the monarch's fufceptibility,
as foon brought him out again, that he
might difclofe his grief to HELOISE.

Her

Her affection for him was not founded on the tottering basis of wealth and ambition, and therefore he had as little reason to fear from the rivalry of a Prince as from that of a peasant, *so far as her constancy was concerned.* And, if her *vanity* was a *little* flattered, (by the consequence which so dazzling a conquest might give her) yet her *heart* was sincerely *alarmed,* when she considered the *power of* her new admirer: to MONTMORIN, therefore, she proposed the scheme of *affected indisposition.* The plan was eagerly embraced by a lover, on the rack of jealousy, as what could *alone* retrieve his own imprudent conduct, in having suffered his Sove-

reign.

reign to contemplate the beauties of his miftrefs.

Matters being thus concerted, he returned to his chamber, where, throwing himfelf on his couch, he in vain endeavoured to procure repofe: fleep was, for the greateft part of the night, banifhed from his eyes, by the undefcribable agitation of his mind; at length, however, *exhaufted nature* funk into *apparent* forgetfulnefs.

But the diftracting idea of being robbed of all that his foul held moft dear, could not be driven from his imagination; his *dreams*, therefore, though

though varied in *circumſtantials*, yet were moſt painfully *uniform* as to their *ſubjeĉt*. At one time they repreſented the King, as hurrying HELOISE from his arms by force; at another, ſhe ſeemed to make *faint* reſiſtance, or rather *not to reſiſt at all*; at length, the appearance of AURORA relieved the wretched ſufferer from diſtreſſes merely ideal.

When the Lord of the caſtle roſe from his couch, he comforted himſelf with reflecting that the *moſt* afflicting part of his *dreaming diſtreſſes* could not be realized, becauſe he could not ſuſpect the conſtancy of HELOISE; but then

then he knew that she might forcibly be torn from him by the rude hand of power: it was now, however, time to cut short all reflections, and to prepare for the necessary attendance on the King, whose repose had been nearly as much disturbed as that of his host.

C H A P.

C H A P. III.

MONTMORIN having received a fummons to attend in the apartment of his royal vifitor, haftened to the levee---from whence he waited on him to the great hall, where breakfaft was prepared. Here the King's difappointment but too plainly betrayed itfelf in his looks, when on cafting his eyes eagerly around, he difcovered the abfence of HELOISE.

To

To Lady MONTMORIN he expreſſed
himſelf much grieved at the va-
cancy in the beautiful circle; and being informed that her abſence was
cauſed by illneſs, he expreſſed an
anxiety which put the Baron's ſoul *on
the rack.*

Breakfaſt being ended, the King
and his ſuite, accompanied by MONT-
MORIN, proceeded to take the diver-
ſion of hunting; and on their return
to the caſtle, many and anxious were
the royal enquiries after the health of
HELOISE: which the monarch had
the ſore mortification to learn was
conſiderably worſe.

When

When the hour of reft arrived, and the King found himfelf again alone with FRONTIN, he fatisfied his impatient longings after intelligence concerning the fair engroffer of his affections; and happy was he to find that her fituation was rather a dependant one, which circumftance ferved to cherifh his hopes of fuccefs;---and after revolving in his mind the moft probable means of accomplifhing his project, he at length determined, that *(at the moment of their departure)* FRONTIN fhould feign himfelf violently ill, and, on this pretence, remain for fome days an inhabitant of the caftle.

The monarch flattered himfelf that FRONTIN's prolonged ftay might afford a favourable opportunity of conveying to HELOISE information of the brilliant conqueft fhe had made. This fcheme being finally agreed on, the confident was difmiffed;--on the next morning, (after acknowledging the hofpitalities of the caftle) the King prepared to depart, when, juft as he was croffing the draw-bridge, the preconcerted indifpofition of FRONTIN took place; his fits were violent, and his royal mafter, (with a well-feigned regret) left him to the care of Lady MONTMORIN.

The

The departure of a kingly vifitor is the removal of a great incumbrance, even from the family of a fubject of the firft rank; but *that* riddance was, comparatively, trifling to MONTMO-RIN, who parted, at once, with a rival and a royal gueft.

With refpect to the illnefs of FRON-TIN, the Baron had, however, his doubts, which determined him to pre-clude the fuppofed invalid from all in-tercourfe in the caftle, except with his own confidential valet. In a remote, but fpacious apartment, therefore, he entertained the *fufpected fpy*, who was

at-

attended by a fervant entirely devoted
to the Baron's intereft.

After a melancholy and ineffuctual
fejour of three days, FRONTIN could
difcover that *he himfelf* was watched;
and that *therefore* he could not render
any fervice to his employer; accordingly, he rapidly recovered his former
health, and bid adieu to the fcene of
his voluntary confinement; leaving the
caftle, poffeffed of no one piece of intelligence, which he had not acquired
before the King's departure, excepting
only that the Baron and HELOISE were
fuppofed to cherifh a reciprocal attachment for each other.

FRON-

FRONTIN's leaving his ftation re-
ftored in a good meafure, to the breaft
of MONTMORIN, its accuftomed tran-
quillity; and fome weeks elapfed
undiftinguifhed by any remarkable
event.

This *calm,* was, however, ruffled
moft unexpectedly, by the arrival of a
courier with a letter from the King,
couched in terms the moft flattering,
and appointing MONTMORIN to the
command of the troops which he was
on the point of fending to the relief of
RHODES.

The

The Baron was at no lofs to account for this *honorable (but moſt unſeaſonable)* exile; fo chagrined was he by this infidious offer, that, at the firſt, he hefitated whether or not he fhould accept it. Violent was the ftruggle between love and honour; on the one hand, the rifque of lofing HELOISE; on the other, the idea of fhewing himſelf unworthy of her, by a daftardly refufal of an honorable command.

In this perplexity, to HELOISE he applied for counfel.----She (with a heroifm not fo marvellous in *her* days, as it would be in *ours*) determined his choice

choice by faying, " if you go," the torch of love will light you in the path of glory; and I will, in your ab- fence, retire to the protection of my aunt (Abbefs of the Paraclete). *There* I will await, with an anxiety which words can but poorly exprefs, the return of my beloved, from the field. Reft affured (added fhe) that my love for your honour, it is, which *alone* could fupport me in the profpect of this tem- porary feparation; and that my attach- ment to you is much too deeply rooted to be fhaken by the hand of power, or the rude blaft of adverfity. She clofed her counfel with remarking, that " ab-

" *abfence leffens a moderate paffion, but feeds a great one,* like the wind which extinguiſhes a taper, but kindles a conflagration."

This ſpeech had its due weight with the *wavering* Baron, who notified to the King his ready acceptance of the appointment with which he was honoured, and declared, that he waited but for *orders to embark.*

To the advice of the heroical HELOISE her lover liſtened the more readily, becauſe the Baron de VALLANCE was at that time impriſoned,

on

on account of fome ouvert acts of fedition. The effects of which would, probably, for a long feafon, incapacitate him from offering any violence to the Houfe of MONTMORIN.

C H A P.

C H A P.   IV.

N OT many days were fuffered to elapfe before the generous HELOISE, having procured a proper difguife, fet off at midnight *for the Paraclete.*

MONTMORIN was her only companion, and after a journey of fomewhat more than two days, they arrived fafely at the wifhed for habitation of her aunt.

At

At the caftle, her departure occafioned the utmoft confufion. Lady
MONTMORIN immediately fufpecting
the Baron of having fecreted HE-
LOISE; at the fame time fhe was un-
able to account for fuch a ftep, as the
King's partiality to her, was a fecret into
which no one there had ever dived.

The Baron having fettled his fair
fugitive under the care of the Abbefs,
haftened to embark for RHODES.
Thither we fhall leave him to purfue
his voyage, and turn our attention to the
King, who delayed not an hour to avail
himfelf of the opportunity, afforded
(as he fuppofed by his rival's abfence)

to

*to pu∫h his favourite plan on to per-
fection.*

To the ca∫tle of MONTMORIN he
repaired without lo∫s of time, under
pretext of intimidating, by his pre-
∫ence, the turbulent va∫∫als of the ∫e-
ditious VALLANCE; who, on the im-
pri∫onment of their Lord had given
∫ome proofs of a tendency to in-
∫urrection.

In∫tantly after the King's arrival at
the ca∫tle, the royal vi∫itor repeated
his enquiries after HELOISE. The
news of her flight enraged him to the
utmo∫t; and cau∫ed a mo∫t pa∫∫ionate
avowal.

avowal of his attachment. The en-
raged Monarch refolved to ranfack
every corner of his dominion till he
fhould difcover the place of her retreat.
To the Lady MONTMORIN he gave it
in charge to tranfmit to him minutely
and expeditioufly, every intelligence
fhe fhould be able to procure concerning the late elopement.

From PARIS, whither he then returned, he fent the ftricteft orders to
every fea-port in his kingdom, to
prevent, (if poffible) the efcape of
HELOISE.

Mean-

Meanwhile, she wrote a letter to Lady Montmorin, replete with affection and gratitude, and expressing the most ardent good wishes for the prosperity of the noble family, under whose patronage the helpless orphan had been blessed with the tenderest attentions. She urged, that *indifpenfable* neceffity had *caufed*, and would, one day, *fully vindicate*, the withdrawing herself from Montmorin; that she was *then* safe in the retirement of a convent, where she proposed to remain until a change of circumstances should render it prudent for her to appear, once more, in the little circle of her honoured friends. The Confeffor of the

the Paraclete conveyed this packet by a peafant, who was prohibited to enter the precincts of the caftle, being ordered to repair thither in the evening, and to throw the letter over the moat.

Having executed his commiffion, the meffenger returned to his employer; the packet that he carried, fully accounted to Lady Montmorin for the King's outrageous behaviour on hearing of the departure of Heloise. With his Majefty's paffion it feemed probable, that fhe herfelf had long been acquainted, and as his defigns muft be confidered as *not honourable*; *therefore* to the virtuous education be-

D   ftowed

ftowed on the fair fugitive (independent
of any pre-engagement of affections)
the Baronefs afcribed the prefent conduct of HELOISE.

The myfterious manner in which
this intelligence was conveyed, led
Lady MONTMORIN to fuppofe, that
her young friend was fecreted fome-
where in the neighbourhood of the
caftle; and ferved totally to preclude
all ideas of her having taken refuge in
fo diftant an afylum as the Paraclete.

The Baronefs (though in a degree
difinclined to her fon's intermarriage
with a perfon not diftinguifhed by nobility

bility of birth) yet felt the utmoft ab-
horrence, at the idea of her amiable
ward's being forced into the toils of
royal feduction.

To the King, therefore, fhe did not
communicate the letter, or any part of
its intelligence. He had not, how--
ever, quitted her caftle, without firft
fecuring in his intereft a domeftic of
the family, from whom he received an
afcount of the purport of that packet.

C H A P. V.

THE Monarch, whofe patience had been nearly exhaufted by a feries of fruitlefs refearches (made at every port in FRANCE) began now to flatter himfelf with fome hopes of fuccefs. He prudently refolved to fcrutinize narrowly the receffes of all the convents in his territories, efpecially of thofe that were adjacent to MONT-MORIN.

Re-

Regard to decorum, however, in-duced him to conceal under a *specious pretence*, the true caufe of this general and accurate enquiry. To this end, the Baron D'Anois, (one of the Nobles who had attended the King on his firft vifit to Montmorin, and who *there* confequently had become acquainted with the perfon of Heloise) was di-rected to fecrete his only daughter, a rich heirefs, then in her thirteenth year.

A folemn and formal application was next made, for the royal per-miffion to examine every convent throughout the dominions of France,

under

under pretence, that her great and independent wealth had rendered the fair fubject of this fearch a prey to fome avaricious procurefs in the caufe of cloyftered devotion; and that fhe would probably be kept immured in the darkfome abode of fequeftered piety, until her affumption of the veil fhould have effectually infured to the convent the poffeffion of her eftate.

The plan was plaufible, and, as fuch, it was put into practice: *fictitious intelligence* comes whenfoever it is wanted; accordingly news foon arrived, that ferved as a pretext to commence the fearch, and it began not far

from

from the caftle whence HELOISE had
efcaped.

The conductor of the fcrutiny carried on his inveftigation through the
whole vicinage of MONTMORIN---in
vain had he fearched all the neighbouring religious foundations, when
the Paraclete was, by one of his confidential attendants, pointed out as the
probable refidence of *her* for whom *he*
really fought.

The uncommon veneration in which
this convent was held, rendered fome
(more than ordinary) formalities *ex-*
pedient, if not *neceffary,* in any attempt

to

to violate the fecrecy of its precinɛts. Accordingly, the Baron (having explained to the Abbefs the *oftenfible* caufe of his vifit, and prefented to her the King's letter, addreffed to, and counterfigned by the Bifhop of the diocefe, folicited her permiffion to fee every inhabitant of the convent.

At the grate there appeared, therefore, *unveiled, all* the members of the houfe; that *no one* was fecreted, the Lady Abbefs folemnly confirmed by the requifite oath. The unconfcious HELOISE prefented her fair face, *without reluɛtance,* becaufe, *without fuf-picion.*

No.

No fooner had the Baron defcried her, than he delivered to her a letter from his mafter, overflowing with pro-feffions of inviolable and ardent at-tachment: fupplicating her to accept his heart, and to complete his felicity, by accompanying his faithful D'Anois to Paris, where it fhould be the un-ceafing bufinefs of his life to make her the *happieft*, as fhe was *the moft lovely* of her fex.

Heloise (after a curfory reading of the letter) cooly and firmly replied, that her birth rendered her by no means a proper partner for a throne; but fhe flattered herfelf both it and her *education*

might

might have fcreened her from *infult*; that in her opinion, " *innocence was a treafure infinitely too valuable to be bartered away, in exchange for the counterfeit gaiety, and artificial happinefs of fplendid ignominy.*"

The groveling mind of D'Anois was little prepared for the reception of fo *dignified* an anfwer to his *dazzling* though *debafing* propofal: but the foul of one who embarks in *fuch a bufinefs*, is already fufficiently funk, to ufe *any* expedient whatever that may promife fuccefs. Accordingly, partly from fear of incurring the royal difpleafure,

in

in cafe of failure, and partly, from
the certain expectation of lofing that
reward of his fervices which his
imagination had painted in glowing
colours---the Baron determined, that
force fhould affift his own, *too feeble
eloquence.*

Againft this premeditated outrage
the vigilance and magnanimity of the
Lady Abbefs provided effectually.---
She *fpiritly obferved* that HELOISE had
on *her*, a double claim for protection;
and therefore, that *without her own
confent*, fhe fhould never leave thofe
walls, raifed for the facred purpofe of
affording

affording an aſſylum to *perſecuted or to deſerted innocence.*

D'Anois entertained too delicate a ſenſe of the danger to·which (*in thoſe days*) all perſons expoſed themſelves, who provoked the complaints of cloyſtered ſocieties; to puſh matters on to extremity, he therefore was conſtrained to return, and relate to his anxious employer the failure of his plan.

The mind of Heloise was, mean-while, torn with inexpreſſible diſ-quietudes. She dreaded, leſt her en-raged and diſappointed ſuitor, armed

as

as he was with regal power, might be tempted to *break down, or to over-leap* all the barriers with which religious reverence, and public opinion, had defended the retreats of a convent: or *at the leaft*, fhe dreaded the difmal confequences which might enfue to her generous protectrefs, in cafe of her perfeverance in the noble line of conduct fhe had hitherto pur-fued. Flight from the Paraclete, and a participation of her lover's lot (whatever that might be) prefented themfelves to her diftracted mind, as preferable, on the whole, to any other plan. In calamitous circumftances, it is furely wifdom to catch comfort

where

where one can, and what *fublunary* comfort more defireable to her, than the fociety of a protector, fuch as MONTMORIN ? She therefore refolved *not* to liften to any fuggeftion *of fear*, but to repair directly to the ifle of RHODES.

This determination will probably be, by fome perfons, condemned as *rafh in the extreme*, whilft others (and thofe the beft judges) will afcribe the conduct of our heroine to that *true magnanimity* which ftoops to no power, and is fhaken by no adverfity; which, by its own peculiar luftre, adorns and heightens every other virtue, and ren-

ders

ders its dignified fubject little folici-
tous about the decifion of judges who
confider men's actions as *blank rhimes*,
to which every one may apply what
fenfe he pleafes.

Actuated neither by *whim* nor *ca-*
price, nor even entirely by her *own at-*
tachment, but under the guidance of
genuine greatnefs of foul, fhe refolved
to leave a country, though her native
one, which too probably could not
long afford to her *honour* a fafe afylum: wifdom and love confpired to
raife, and to fuftain her mind on this
arduous occafion, and to *what* exertions is not humanity equal, when
thus directed, and *thus* fupported?

C H A P.

C H A P.   VI.

HELOISE, her plan once formed, delayed *not* for a moment the execution of it. The porter of the convent was foon bribed into her intereft, and fhe took leave of her cloyfter, immediately after mattins next morning. For companion of her flight, fhe had a guide whom the door-keeper procured for her; and they directed their fteps by the light of a bright moon to a neighbouring vil-lage. There the amiable and accom-

plifhed

plifhed fugitive affumed the appearance
of a minftrel, for which difguife her
mufical talents well fitted her. Equiped
in her new chara&er, fhe purfued her
journey to the next fea-port, and in a
few days found herfelf, for the firft
time, within fight of the ocean.

The feelings and the apprehenfions
of a young and delicate female, thus
circumftanced, will hardly admit of
an adequate defcription.

Umpire of her own fate, and fove-
reign of her own a&ions, without the
aid of any counfellor :---Of that pru-
dence, which is the refult of experience,

E   fhe

she could not possess a large stock;
but duty to herself, and passion for
her lover, conspired to *point out her
path*. The novelty of the scene before
her excited admiration; whilst the idea,
that the widely extended abyss, rolled
its countless waves between her and the
object of her fondest regard, tempted
her to despair.

The die was, now cast; the *first* opportunity was therefore to be embraced, of committing herself to the
faithless element. A transport laden
with military stores for RHODES lay at
the quay, ready to slip her cables;
the guide was rewarded, and dismissed;

her

her paffage was agreed for, and (in a few hours after her arrival at the fea-fide) the magnanimous minftrel was launched upon the deep.

For the firft day and night the wind and weather were propitious; on the fecond morning they both altered un-favourably, and continued adverfely tempeftuous for a week; the fufferings of the lovely wanderer during this dreary feafon of mental agitation, and of extreme inconvenience, were fuch as would irremediably have funk a fpirit lefs elevated and firm. Nothing con-tributed more to the diftrefs of her mind, on this occafion, than an ap-

pre-

prehenfion that the winds and waves *might be found to fight againft her*; by driving the veffel back into a FRENCH harbour.

Thefe fears of HELOISE, were, on the ninth day of the voyage, fadly realized; for, whilft feated penfive on the deck, and occupied, in ruminating on this fad reverfe of fortune (being now arrived at the Pier) fhe was awakened from her reverie by the chilling appearance of D'ANOIS : he, on a fecond vifit to the Paraclete had, by promifes of indemnity, and an immenfe bribe, learned from the porter every particular relative to the *de-*

parture,

parture, *difguife*, and probable *deftina-*
tion of the lovely wanderer. Her guide
was fent for to the Baron's quarters,
near the convent, where the *principles*
of loyalty were found abfolutely neceffary to be called forth, and their in-
fluence *added* to a confiderable reward,
before D'Anois could extract from
him the certain knowledge of every
minute circumftance of the embark-
ation. This poor peafant had a mind
fuperior to his condition, and could at
laft be induced to reveal his employer's
fecret, *only* by an affurance, (to which
he gave credit) that a treafon of the
blackeft dye, againft the life of the

Mo-

Monarch, was the charge on which the fugitive was to be arrefted.

D'Anois, no longer in doubt as to the meafures to be taken, purfued the fteps of Heloise, determining to carry on the chace, on the fea, as well as on the land, in the moft expeditious manner poffible. The contrary and boifterous winds had detained him on the rack, till the morning of the tranf-port's putting back; great was his joy when he beheld his plan advancing fo fuccefsfully, on being told by the mafter of the veffel, that a minftrel, in every refpect anfwering his defcrip-tion, was at that moment upon deck.

Thither

Thither he flew to fecure his prey: the fight of him quite overpowered the hitherto unfhaken mind of HELOISE, who (whilft yet in a fainting fit) was hurried on fhore by her vigilant and indefatigable purfuer.

D'ANOIS was the firft object that prefented itfelf to her half opening eyes;---he now affumed all the appearances of foothing and fympathizing regard: He fet before her, what *he* called the *happinefs* of her efcaping from the completion of a plan, fo *rafh*, and fo *degrading*, and which would, probably, have proved *difgufting* alfo to him fhe ought. He then proceeded to ridicule

E 4 her

her ideas of right and wrong, which
she juftly confidered as in their nature
immutable; and affured her, with many
eloquent fhrugs, that ladies were honored,
not difgraced, by granting favours to
Kings. He urged, that the higheft
rank, with fuitable opulence, now
awaited her; whilft, in cafe of ob-
ftinate refufal of the proffered happinefs, and enviable diftinctions, fhe
could not expect the enjoyment of
her *liberty*; for, that her Monarch
might be hurt by the *avowed pre-
ference* given by his *fubject* to his
rival.

To

To thefe arguments HELOISE lif-
tened with filent difdain---her *foul* was
calm and ferene; fhe faid, that in form-
ing her plan, fhe had fuffered much,
from perturbations, *how* beft to efcape
from *titled infamy*; but that, to *thofe
troubles*, an happy calm had fucceeded,
which enabled her to judge of her prefent perilous fituation; and that for a
mind well principled, a prifon, *unat-
tended by guilt*, had no fuch horrors as
thofe, with which fhe unaffectedly
thought of the refidence of a *King's
miftrefs*.

HELOISE then refolutely *demanded
her freedom*---to this D'ANOIS replied,

that

that fhe who could command a great
Monarch had little reafon to regret
being reftrained from deftroying her
own happinefs; adding, that if ever
her royal lover fhould betray any in-
conftancy; or if, at any very remote
period of life, fhe herfelf fhould wifh
to retire from the world, fhe might
return to her beloved Paraclete in
the *exalted rank of Lady Abbefs.*

HELOISE, incenfed to the utmoft, at
his laft outrageous infult, replied with
indignation, " Think not, that after
I fhould have once forfaken the paths
of Virtue, I could expect fupport,
(under my *weight of woe*) from any
elevation,

elevation that is only advantageous to those who have *not* bartered away principle in exchange for any *other* good; and you may be assured, that your base business is *not* the nearer to a successful issue, because you have obtained the custody of my person:--my *mind* is still *free*, and will continue so; and my affections *will* never, *can* never, submit to the *power* of that despicable despot who disgraces by thus employing you. Desist therefore from attempting to execute what your heart must condemn; blush at what you have done, for where *there is shame*, there *may* be *virtue*.

The

The difheartened D'Anois, full of perplexity, and half afhamed of his embaffy, retired from Heloise, hav-firft carefully fecured her door. After the abfence of a few hours this unfuc-cefsful pleader returned to his charge, and informed her that, on the follow-ing morning, he fhould conduct her to Paris. He then preffed her to accept of fome refrefhments, of which fhe partook fparingly and filently. This done, he took his leave, with expreffions of much politenefs, and with fentiments of more real re-fpect than he had ever before enter-tained *for any female whatever.*

C H A P.

C H A P. VII.

HELOISE had not spent her so-
litary time that day, *merely as an hope-
less prisoner in the Bastille*, in revolving
the adventures of her life, and in think-
ing what might hereafter be the sequel
of her tragic story; but she devoted
part of her attention to a strict examination of the situation and strength
of her prison. She soon perceived
that the upright iron bars of the windows in the bedchamber were inserted
in frames less strong than those of the

outer

outer room; and that with the help of a knife, one of them might eafily be removed from its decayed focket.

Thefe ufeful obfervations were made before fhe had partaken of her fparing repaft, and no fooner had her defpicable jailor wifhed her a night of undifturbed repofe, than fhe proceeded to avail herfelf of the difcovery fhe had made refpecting the windows.

As foon as fhe had effected the removal of the window-bar, fhe was able, by looking commodioufly out of the cafement, to explore the fituation of her place of confinement. She

had

had now the fatisfaction to find, that as her prifon-houfe was built on the very rampart, if fhe could, by any means, defcend from her window, and reach the ground *unhurt*, fhe might poffibly effect an efcape : this plan fhe accordingly accomplifhed by means of D'ANOIS fafh, which he had left in the room.

HELOISE having accuftomed herfelf to fmaller dangers, had increafed her intrepidity, and fitted her mind for meeting greater ones : ignorant of the country where fhe now found herfelf---at a lofs whither to fly---guided by the roaring of the billows, fhe directed her

fteps

steps to the beach. There the amiable
wanderer encountered a person, who,
in the event proved, the master of a
vessel then in the offing, which waited
but *his* presence to slip her cable. To
his enquiries, respecting her destination,
and the cause of her present nocturnal
ramble, HELOISE made answer, that
" having arrived too late to procure
admission into the town, she had been
constrained to await, unhoused, the
approach of day, when she hoped to
procure a passage for RHODES, whither she was bound.

The great estimation in which the
minstrels of those times were held by
all

all ranks, the idea that their characters
were, in fome fort, facred, the elegant
entertainment their company never
failed to afford, in an age not abound-
ing with elegance of any fort, induced
the mafter to make offer of a place in
his veffel to the fictitious bard, who
joyfully embracing fo defirable an opportunity of eluding the refearches of
her purfuers, once more committed
herfelf to the *faithlefs element*. A few
hours wafted her from the fhores of
FRANCE, and a favourable gale ferved
gradually to *diffipate her apprehenfions*;
whilft D'ANOIS (on difcovering the
flight of HELOISE) became quite defperate; and, dreading the refentment

F   of

of his difappointed employer, he rafhly terminated, by his own hand, a life, devoted to the equally cruel and ignominious purfuits of feduction; a conduct for which he could not even urge the flimfy extenuation of an ungoverned paffion of *his own.* The King, meanwhile, confoled himfelf for the lofs of HELOISE, by the fociety of D'ANOIS' *orphan daughter,* whofe unprotected condition rendered her an eafy victim to the royal defigns.

It nearly concerns all who lay fnares for female innocence, to confider, that the time *may* come, when (at the expence of their own nearest and deareft

con-

connections) the law of retaliation may
be put in execution againſt themſelves;
and however the vanity that *inſpires,* may
varniſh over the cruel act of ſeduction,
yet, in the unavoidable moments of
reflection it will appear in its true
colours, and as the certain fore-runner
of events equally fatal to individuals,
and to ſociety at large.

CHAP.

C H A P. VIII.

No one would be *more* unhappy than a perfon who had *never* known adverfity, which, whoever bears *properly*, (in fome fort) may be faid to *deferve* profperity.

HELOISE was fupported, by confidering, that each wave wafted her nearer to her gallant lover; while he was employed in reaping laurels on the fhore of RHODES, at the memorable fiege of a city, reckoned one of the feven

won-

wonders of the world; and which had, two hundred years before that time, been refcued out of the poffeffion of the SARACENS, by the Knights of JERU-SALEM.

MONTMORIN fhared largely in the applaufe beftowed on the glorious exertions of public fpirit, and the nearly unequalled proofs of perfonal prowefs, which confpired to give deathlefs fame to the defenders of RHODES.

. No fooner was the projected fiege of this city publickly known, than EUROPE beheld the flower of her nobility, crowding with enthufiafm, to

pur-

purchafe military glory under the ram-parts of RHODES, whofe relief was helped forward by the various jarring interefts of European Princes; for it is a juft obfervation, that turbulent bufy fpirits are more eafily *evaporated* than *confined.*

A potent Ariftocracy at home had at that period confiderably weakened *each* Monarch in Europe; therefore *all* Monarchs faw, that it was their *common* intereft, and each one felt it to be his own *particular* intereft, to cut out *diftant work for formidable Barons.* Thefe petty tyrants were in moft cafes found as *oppreffive* to the lower orders, as

dan-

dangerous to their Sovereigns, againſt whoſe power they inveighed with a *bitterneſs,* generally proportioned to the *deſpotiſm* they themſelves practiſed on their own dependents.

To the genius of *Cruſade,* therefore, were the Sovereigns of EUROPE much indebted for their deliverance from the encroachment of powerful ſubjects, who thought " they had a *right* to as much liberty as *they could get.*"

The reigning Grand-maſter, D'AU-BUSSON, provided with celerity, for a vigorous defence; accordingly the infidel army, on its firſt appearance off

this

this ifland found a city prepared to refift the attacks of a more formidable foe. In aid of thefe exertions were to be reckoned the gallant enthufiafm of the times; and laftly, papal indulgences granted (with a lavifh hand by Sixtus the Fourth, at the inftance of Lewis the Eleventh of France) to all who fhould contribute *pecuniary affiftance* to the Knights of RHODES, whofe coffers (exhaufted by perpetual and unprofit- able wars) were thus fpeedily and amply replenifhed.

It was in the end of APRIL that the Turkifh fleet was defcried in the Off- ing, ftanding in for the fhore : a heavy

can-

canonade foon commenced, which was
brifkly returned by the citadel, and
from the ramparts of RHODES: after
fuftaining a long action, the enemy,
though with very great difficulty, effected a landing, both of cavalry and
infantry ; and thefe troops fpeedily in-
trenched themfelves on the hill of Saint
STEPHEN, on which their batteries
were no fooner mounted, and well
appointed, than the city was fummoned
to furrender. But *promifes* and *threats*
proving alike ineffectual, the horfe
made a fally from their intrenchments,
and came up to the very gates. Of
this excurfion, they had, however, foon
caufe to repent; for MONTMORIN, at
the

the head of a fquadron of light cavalry, making a *fortee*, routed and purfued them to the very ditch of their camp. Among the flain on this occafion was found the notorious renegado DEME-TRIUS, who fell, *not* by the fword of the purfuers, but by the accident of his horfe ftumbling in fight, and his own troops riding over him.

MONTMORIN returned unhurt him-felf, and with a very inconfiderable lofs of his men, fave only the death of a gallant Knight, named MURAT, a cadet of the illuftrious houfe of Le TOURS.

The

The befiegers, wearied with re-peated and indecifive fkirmifhes, em-ployed a GERMAN engineer (who had been long in their fervice) to recon-noitre, and to advife how beft to direct the whole fire of their artillery. This tafk was foon accomplifhed, and the Bafhaw PALEOLOGUE pointed his bat-teries (by the renegado's advice) againft the tower of St. NICOLAS. The Turkifh Generaliffimo was at the fame time, flattered by affurances, that under *his* aufpices, an attack *fo conducted*, would foon difplay the crefent on the battle-tlements of RHODES.

The

The Grand-master, with a vigilance
equal to his valour, ufed every effort
to drive the Turks from their guns,
and to difmantle their fortifications ;
and although he was *not quite* fuccefsful
in his endeavours, yet he foon convinced the affailants that *they* had been
led, to form expectations, much too
fanguine, as to the event of their engineer's plan.

Of the ftrength of *one* tower in particular, experience convinced them,
they had thought by far too meanly.
A council of war was then held, the
refult of which was a determination to
fend this fame engineer as a fpy into
the

the town, to form an accurate opinion concerning the feveral baftions.

The faithlefs German readily agreed to act his part, and accordingly prefented himfelf before the ramparts in a pofture fuited to his pretences. MONTMORIN happened to be the firft officer who obferved him, and he afforded protection to the deferter; but it was with a hand *half* extended, and *half* drawn back.

To the Grand-mafter the cautious Baron inftantly conveyed this fufpected convert. D'AUBUSSON was then fitting in council with his principal com-

manders,

manders; to them the German pro-
feſſed the deepeſt compunction for
the part he had taken againſt the
Chriſtians, moſt humbly ſuing for re-
admiſſion into the boſom of the church,
and for ſome military employment,
whoſe labours and perils might bring
his ſincerity ſpeedily to the trial.

The *religious* part of his petition
was immediately granted; but he was
ſtrictly watched, becauſe greatly ſuſ-
pected. On his examination he endeavoured to inſpire the Knights with
high ideas of the *force, appointments,*
and *determined reſolution* of the enemy.
Theſe artifices being ſeen through,
could

could not fail to operate againft his employers; and *that* day's council of war rofe with a fpirit of increafed refolution : *Death* or *Victory* were the only alternatives with its determined members.

After little more than a week, the German was detected in conveying intelligence to the Turks, by means of a letter tied to an arrow; and he next day received the reward of his villainy, from the hand of his executioner.

With an almoft inceffant firing from the batteries, the befiegers laboured

to

to effect a breach, which defign they accomplifhed on the ninth of *June*. Their fury was inftantly directed to the tower of St. Nicholas; its fhattered condition encouraging them to hope that it would become an eafy prey: but there they were again difappointed; for this poft was *fo* dangerous and *fo* important, that it had attracted the attention, and infured the perfonal fervice of the moft experienced, and moft valiant commanders of the order.

The command of the chofen band, which occupied this tower, was fhared between the grand-mafter and two others,

others, of moft diftinguifhed emi-
nence; his brother, the Vifcount
D'Aubusson, and the Baron Montmorin.

C H A P. IX.

THE *Turks*, although the sur-
rounding atmofphere feemed kindled
into a conflagration, in a frenzy of
contagious courage, fcimeter in hand,
fix and afcend their ladders, as if totally infenfible of the unremitting fire
directed at them from all parts.

Probably the fury, and the perfeverance, which on that occafion united
in the affailants, would have proved too
hard

hard for any *defenders* but the Knights
of JERUSALEM.

MONTMORIN, who had early recom-
mended himfelf to the favour of the
grand-mafter, by fighting at his fide,
on this, as on every other occafion,
difplayed the moft intrepid valour.
CARETTI, one of the *Commanders* be-
longing to the order, ftanding clofe to
them when D'AUBUSSON loft his hel-
met, refpectfully intreated him to retire; he was anfwered, " *This* is the
poft of honor, *here,* and *no where elfe*;
therefore, fhould your Grand-mafter be
feen. If I fall, you have much more
to hope, than I to fear."

G 2   The

The *eye*, and the *example* of such a leader, could not fail to raise such troops above the ordinary standard of military exertion. Towards the close of the action, the gallant heroes found themselves surrounded with a sort of rampart, raised by their own valour, and composed of the bodies of the slain.

The assailants now rendered quite desperate by the obstinate resistance of the Knights, endeavoured, by means of strong iron hooks, fixed to very large cables, to *pull those heroes down from the battlements*, that they might slaughter them in the trenches.

The

The grand-mafter himfelf was feized on by one of thefe hooks, and was dragged to the *brow of the precipice*, when his faithful MONTMORIN fevered the cable with one ftroke of his battle axe; then, with a well aimed arrow, he transfixed the breaft of the Turk who held the rope.

His bravery and conduct on this occafion ferved to raife him ftill higher in the efteem of the Knights, and in the friendfhip of the illuftrious hero, whofe life he had faved, and from whom (on condition of his affuming the habit of the order) he received the offer of a ftation at once *elevated and*

lucra-

lucrative. But here, the tender re-
membrance of the beloved HELOISE
interpofed, and effectually precluded
his acceptance of any advantage or
dignity *connected with celibacy.*

On the twenty-fixth day of July,
the infidels, who had now loft a very
confiderable portion of their army, began and kept up a heavy fire againft
the *Jews'* quarter of the town: this attack continued with unremitting fury
for twenty-four hours; at the expira-
tion of that time a breach was made,
at which, however, the impetuous affailants were not fuffered to enter.
At this critical juncture the Grand-
mafter

mafter haftened to difplay the ftandard of the crofs, an expedient to which recourfe was never had but in cafes of the extremeft neceffity.

The befieged, re-animated at this fight, returned to the charge with double ardour; they had, however, foon the mortification to behold the Turks become mafters of the breach. The Bafhaw, who had before this, laid a plan for poifoning the Grand-mafter, now fet an immenfe price on his head; accordingly, twelve Janiffaries undertook to *cut their way to* D'AUBUSSON, and they effected their defperate enterprize.

This

This gallant leader, of the uncon-
quered Knights, received from them
five wounds at once, and for near a
minute, he was unaffifted by his brave
comrades; but his brother the Vifcount, happily at the moment of the
exigency, reinforcing that part of the
garrifon, cut the Janiffaries to pieces,
and feized their holy ftandard, which
had been planted in the breach.

This revolution in their affairs being
obferved by the befiegers, they fled in
wild difmay. MONTMORIN obferving
their flight (and being animated with
an ardour, which the long continuance
of the battle had *encreafed*, rather than
abated)

abated) was foremoft in the *purfuit,* and followed the fugitives rafhly, until (being furrounded by the retreating foe) he was taken prifoner, and carried on board the Turkifh gallies.

C H A P. X.

H ELOISE, after a tolerable paffage, had arrived within fight of
RHODES : on beholding, with longing
eyes, the wifhed-for fhore, fhe flattered herfelf, that all her troubles were
now fpeedily to ceafe. The incon-
veniences of her voyage had neither
been *few* nor *flight* ; and a very ferious
and perplexing diftrefs had arifen to
her in the courfe of it. An unfortunate difcovery of her fex gave rife to
this---the difficulties refulting from
                                          which

which unlucky accident were of a nature so embarrassing, as to require *all
her quickness,* and all her *firmness of
mind* to surmount them. In return to
repeated and passionate offers of mar-
riage, HELOISE had the address to
make such equivocal returns, as left
the Captain little reason to suppose that
his happiness waited for any thing but
the benediction of the church, which
could not be procured before their arrival at port. To her importunate
lover the fair fugitive had assigned her
attachment to a favorite brother, as the
cause of her disguise, and of her ex-
pedition. She represented her family
at home, as harassed by a powerful
neighbour

neighbour, who availed himfelf of her brother's abfence; and that fhe had taken this, feemingly defperate, refolution with a view of inftantly recalling him from the purfuit of fame at RHODES, to the protection of his widow-mother, and defencelefs orphan fifters *at home.*

The enamoured Captain (whilft indulging himfelf in reveries on his approaching blifs) was roufed to attention by the fight of a Turkifh galley bearing down upon him. The action foon commenced on the part of the *Turks*; and after an unequal conteft

of

of not many minutes, the French fhip
was conftrained to *ftrike her cclours.*

The victors having manned the
veffel from their own crew, conducted
her in triumph to the fhore, where
their fleet lay at anchor.

HELOISE (who immediately on the
difcovery of her fex) had affumed her
proper habit, was, without delay, conveyed to the galley of PALEOLOGUE,
there to await his pleafure. She now
abandoned herfelf, for the firft time,
to the moft poignant grief. Her mind
foftened by the contemplation of expected felicity) was doubly fenfible of
the

the cruel ftroke that diffolved the vifionary charm. Seated at the window of her cabbin, fhe now, with indefcribable anguifh, defcried the walls of RHODES, and her terrors infinuated, that *every fhot the enemy fired,* might deprive MONTMORIN of life.

A prey to thefe cruel reflections, HELOISE remained for fome time, till the memorable defeat of the 27th of JULY determined PALEOLOGUE rather to rifque the effects of MAHOMET's anger, than another rencounter with the Knights.

Accordingly, on the twenty-eighth he embarked, and on the following day spread his sails for his own shore, carrying with him and his ruined army, no other trophies than MONTMORIN (who, with all conceivable indignation rejected the offers made to procure his apostacy) and the unfortunate HELOISE, now sinking under the pressure of an intolerable weight of woe: the idea, that every time the oars divided the briny waves, they bore her still *farther* from all she held most dear, was little short of distracting. In these circumstances, still ignorant of her lover's fate, she received a notification from

the

the Bashaw, that he meant to pass the
night in her cabbin.

PALEOLOGUE, originally a Greek
Christian of the Imperial family of
CONSTANTINOPLE, had so far adopted
the brutal manners of the Turks, that
he made known this intention to his
beautiful captive, without any desire
to *engage her affections*, but merely to
possess her person. To her, this message
was terrible, *in the extreme*; she now
considered her situation as absolutely
desperate, and that *therefore* she was
not only *authorised*, *but called upon* to
have recourse to the most desperate
exertion; accordingly, she resolved that
the

the apostate should pay his life, as the forfeit of his crime.

The Bashaw, on entering the cabbin, found HELOISE, seated on her sofa, with a dagger in her hand :---a sight so uncommon made him start. He ordered his captive to " throw aside that instrument of death." Scarcely had he uttered these words, when a number of mutes appeared, who (by order of the second in command) arrested the unsuspecting Bashaw.

The second in command who had given orders for this arrest, well knew the indignation that MAHOMET would

H   feel

feel againſt PALEOLOGUE, for having raiſed the ſiege; and therefore he determined by this ſtep, to ſecure to himſelf his maſter's favour. On the removal of the fallen Baſhaw, out of the cabbin of HELOISE to his own (where he was ſtrictly guarded) ſhe returned thanks to Heaven for her wonderful delivery; and conſidering this as an earneſt of future help, her ſpirits revived, and ſhe retired to reſt. Unacquainted with the *whole extent* of her preſent good fortune, ſhe knew not that ſhe herſelf was now conſidered as *part* of the *confiſcated* property of her brutal admirer; and that *on this accompt*, her perſon would neceſſarily remain inviolate,

violate, until the Emperor (to whom fhe now devolved) fhould determine her deftiny.

A propitious voyage foon conducted into port the veffel which carried this rich prize, and MAHOMET delayed not long to confirm the difgrace of the Bafhaw, who was, however, permitted to retire into exile, all his poffeffions having been firft configned to the Emperor's ufe.

HELOISE was, within a few days, fent for into the prefence of MAHOMET, who (not being as much fmitten with her as others had been) beftowed her

H 2

on

on the fucceffor of PALEOLOGUE, the very fame officer who had put him under arreft for having given up the fiege; by her new proprietor was the lovely HELOISE conducted to his Haram.

CHAP.

C H A P. XI.

MONTMORIN, in the mean time, was fold to a wealthy Mahome-tan, who, for one part of the year, re-fided at CONSTANTINOPLE, but for the other part, at a villa near the city. This mafter employed his new purchafe in the lowest menial offices of his houfe, in which fituation did feveral tedious months roll over the head of the diftreffed Baron.

H 3   During

During the fiege; the perpetually varying fcenes, the din of arms, and of martial mufic,---thefe had banifhed, in fome degree, from his recollection, the charms of HELOISE; but in the cheerlefs uniform folitude of adverfity, her beloved idea was *more ftrongly* ftamped on his yielding heart than ever.

His fufferings now naturally ferved to awaken in his anxious breaft a thoufand diftreffing apprehenfions on her account, and on that of his family.

Bufinefs is perhaps the very beft human remedy againft forrow; but then it it muſt be a *buſineſs that intereſts the mind*, ſomewhat *more* than did the *occupations* of the unfortunate MONT-MORIN.

Whilſt the penſive captive indulged his melancholy reflections, his maſter afforded him ſome ſmall relief by changing the ſcene of his employment, which was now transferred to the country, where to him was conſigned the care of a garden.

CICERO, ſomewhere ſays, that " the pleaſures of an huſbandman are next to thoſe of a philoſopher;" but then the peaſant muſt *not* be deprived of liberty,

liberty, and he muſt *not* be far removed from his native country, *elſe* his pleaſures will be *few indeed.*

The profound retirement of the villa ſoon became far more irkſome to the love-ſick ſlave, than the laborious life led in the metropolis; and yet, deſperate as matters appear to be, the hour of his delivery drew nigh.

One evening, as MONTMORIN walked alone in the garden, he obſerved a man ſliding down one of the walls; on perceiving that he was diſcovered, he endeavoured to return as he came, but (miſſing his hold) he fell.

fell. In this condition the Baron feized him; when the Turk drawing a dagger from his breaft, threatened his antagonift with inftant death, if he did not quit his hold.

MONTMORIN proving the more alert and able of the combatants, feizing the dagger, difarmed the ftranger, who from the *drefs*, collecting the *condition* of his conqueror, thus addreffed him : " Doubtlefs liberty muft ftill be dear to you; and (if you will affift me in eloping with one of your mafter's wives, who now expects me) I will fupply you with money, and facilitate your return to your native country.

Here,

Here, added he, is a bag of fequins, as an earneft of my future protection, and you may *inftantly* become the companion of my flight."

The propofal was readily accepted, and at the moment, appeaied the expected fair one in the garden. She, and her lover, made their efcape on Arabian fteeds prepared for them, and which foon conveyed them beyond the reach of their purfuers; MONT-MORIN (mounted on the horfe of one of the attendants) being of the party.

In a few hours ABDAD, the adventurous Turk, and his miftrefs, found them-

themfelves at a fmall country retirement, where the mafter of the houfe
treated MONTMORIN with great bene-
ficence, who, after a ftay of three days,
left his hoft and his fultanna happy in
the enjoyment of each other.

Under the direction of a guide, the
Baron bent his courfe towards the fea
coaft; the fun had not rifen when
he left the abode of ABDAD; and he
diligently purfued his route, without
any interruption, until he and his companion were driven, for fhelter, into a
cavern by the road fide.

Here

Here they repofed, till they were (by the evening's lengthening fha-dows) invited to profecute their jour-ney. Night overtaking the travellers on the houfelefs edge of a foreft, they refolved to avail themfelves of its pro-tection, and to pafs their fleeping hours amid the boughs of fome lofty tree, that they might efcape the danger, in thofe regions fo common, of attacks from wild beafts.

A ftately tree prefented itfelf, in the branches of which MONTMORIN was no fooner placed than he extended his hand to the guide, who (in the act of afcending) became the prey of a lion.

This

This beaſt lay ſleeping at the foot
of the tree, and being covered by the
bruſh-wood that ſurrounded it, had
eſcaped the obſervation of the travellers.

Piteous as were the cries of the
guide,---humane and brave as was
MONTMORIN; yet, before any aſſiſt-
ance could poſſibly be attempted, the
motion of the lion's jaws declared the
lamentable fate of the poor Turk.

END OF VOL I.